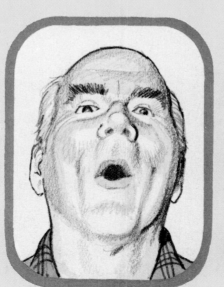

Uncle Josh Stories

Helen C. Noordewier

Steve Bates, *illustrator*

Best Wishes,
Helen C. Noordewier

Baker Book House
Grand Rapids, Michigan 49506

For my sister Claire

Contents

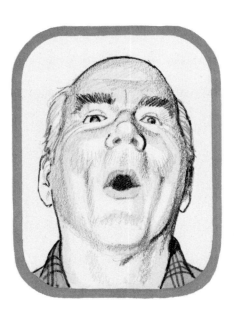

1

The Story Man

Uncle Josh and Aunt Miranda lived in the hills of Kentucky. All of his life Uncle Josh had been a school teacher in a lonely place in Kansas. But when the law said that he was too old to teach he moved back to Kentucky where he had lived when he was a boy. He and Aunt Miranda bought a little home which rested on the top of a high hill.

"Just look now, Mirandy," he had said. "From here we can see the whole valley. Up here we are the king and the queen of all of Kentucky." And when the morning sun said hello to them as it rose behind the cabin, he would say, "Just look at it, Mirandy. We can almost touch it. It's as though it shines for us alone."

There was not much that Uncle Josh and Aunt Miranda needed. One cow gave them all their milk. There was enough land for a giant vegetable garden, and a few chickens laid all the eggs they could use. Along the side of the cabin was a giant apple tree and a long vine which bore so many grapes that Aunt Miranda made grape jelly for the whole year.

"There is only one thing missing, Mirandy," Uncle Josh said.

"Now, what could that be, Joshua?" Miranda asked.

"The children," he said. "It's the children I miss. The little ones, like I used to teach in Kansas."

But a little time took care of that. The children in the valley heard about Uncle Josh and soon found out that his years of teaching school had made him a wonderful story-teller. Throughout the whole valley he got to be known as Uncle Josh, the story man. The children found small reasons for coming up the big hill to the little cabin and they would beg Uncle Josh to tell them a story. Then when they found that Aunt Miranda added to their fun by making hot choco-late and cookies they became regular visitors. There were five of them: David and Seth, Martha and Cecilia, who was called Cee-Cee, and three-year-old Lucretia, whom they called Lulu. She was the tiny one. All of the others went to school.

Their trips to the cabin on the hill were almost always on Saturday morning, but if there was a vacation day from school they always managed an extra visit. Uncle Josh would stand on the porch to welcome them with outstretched arms and Aunt Miranda always made a last-minute appearance at the kitchen door.

"C'mon up, c'mon up!" Uncle Josh would call, and Aunt Miranda's big smile, as she wiped her hands on her apron, was a welcome big enough for anyone.

"Put yourselves down," Uncle Josh would say and if the day was warm and sunny the children would sit in a semicircle on the little porch. But if the winds were cold and snappy, Uncle Josh would say, "Better come in the cabin today. The wind is out to pinch your noses." And then the listening place would be in the kitchen, the old kitchen that always smelled like molasses cookies and applesauce; the old kitchen where the floor creaked a little, but where it was always warm and cozy. And it was there that the story would begin.

Today Uncle Josh could see them coming up the hill. "C'mon up!" he called, as usual, and when the children caught sight of him they began to run.

"It's just as though I am back in that old schoolroom in Kansas," he would say to Miranda. "Children all over the world are the same. Look at them now. They are all motor-driven, Mirandy. Just look at those little legs fly."

"Tell us about your school again, Uncle Josh, tell us about your school," the children shouted.

"All right, all right," Uncle Josh said. "Sit down."

Well, it wasn't like your school, little ones. There were no buses to ride on. Everybody walked, some a mile and some much farther than that. Come winter time it was a pretty cold hike and when I would see them coming, I'd open the door wide and they would begin to run. Right away we would have a nose-wiping session and then the outdoor clothes would come off and everyone would gather around the big old stove. There was a good fire going because I had been there for two hours already and Mirandy had brought me my second cup of coffee. But we had a rule. Once inside of the school the children had to be quiet. They could talk together but only in school voices, as we called them. The shouting was saved for noon hours and recess times, and oh, how they could shout. They were like a flock of birds chirping and shaking their feathers. Remember, this was a one-room school; all eight grades in one room. Sometimes the little ones became a bit restless, waiting for the big ones to get finished with a lesson, but on the whole they did pretty well. Waiting taught them to be patient and that was a worthwhile lesson to learn.

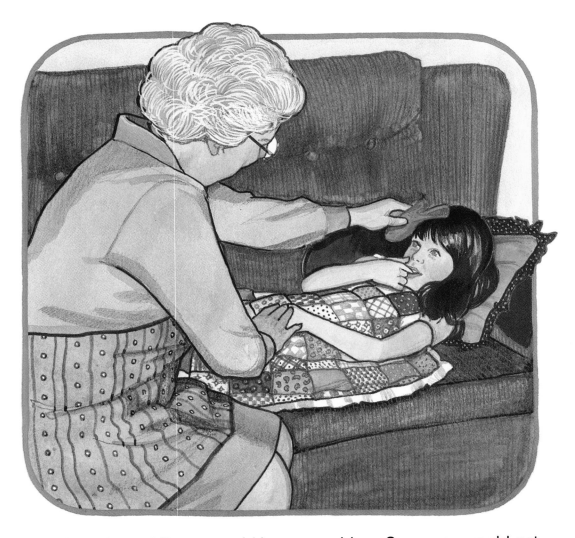

Once in a while we would have a problem. Someone would get sick and I always knew when it was going to happen. In the morning some little child would come with a note from her mama. And usually it said the same thing. Something like this: "Lucy did not feel too well this morning, but I couldn't make her stay home. She likes school so much. Will you please keep an eye on her?"

Well, I knew right away what would happen. By recess time Lucy would be sick and I would have to send her to Mirandy and she would put her on our big old couch. Mirandy got to be a pretty good nurse. But for a while we had a little problem. The little ones thought it was pretty nice to spend the day with Mirandy and they started to play sick. Well, we fixed that too. We made a concoction of a little bit of everything—honey and all kinds of spices—stuff that wouldn't hurt anybody but didn't taste very good. Soon the word got around that if you were going to spend the day with Mirandy, a teaspoon of medicine was part of the deal. Well, that did it. We had no more foolers, and Aunt Mirandy could tell if a child was really sick. Then they got no medicine.

"Did Aunt Mirandy like the children?" Cee-Cee asked.

"Oh, yes, that she did," Uncle Josh answered. "She liked them almost as much as I did."

"And did she like Kansas?" David wanted to know.

"Well now," Uncle Josh said, and he stroked his chin. "Sometimes yes and sometimes no. She didn't like the howling of the wind as it blew across the prairie, or the night howls of the coyotes. And when she went to the pump for a pail of water she wasn't happy when the Kansas wind blew half of it out of the pail before she reached the house. But she liked the people, David, and if you look at Aunt Mirandy's face you can see that she smiled a lot. Just see how the smiling wrinkles circle her mouth and her eyes, and there are no frowning lines on her forehead. Somehow, you know, when you get older your face is the storybook of your life."

"And what about you, Uncle Josh?" Seth asked. "Did you like being a school teacher in Kansas?"

"Oh, yes, my boy, I sure did," Uncle Josh said. "I loved the children and I was happy with their parents, at least with most of them."

They were farmers and they couldn't afford to pay me much when it came to real money, but they paid me in other ways. In the summer there were always fresh vegetables at our back door which someone had dropped off and when it was slaughtering time there was always meat for the teacher. And it was always the good cuts. But there was one thing that Mirandy and I always wished for, and that was a nice piece of liver. One day we told one of the farmers about it. He looked really surprised.

"Liver!" he said. "Liver! We feed that to the pigs!"

So you see, we always had plenty of food and the little house we lived in belonged to the school so we had no rent to pay. Along with the free house there was a barn which housed a balky old horse and beat-up old buggy. That was how we got around from one farm to another, Mirandy and I. And that old horse, well, he was our weather man. When school was over for the day and Mirandy and I were asked to one of the farmer's homes for coffee, I would look at the sky and wonder about the weather. That old buggy wasn't very water-proof and the rain storms in Kansas could be something terrible. Then Mirandy would say, "The horse, Joshua. Go and get the horse. He will tell us about the weather." And he sure did. If it promised to be good he would trot calmly down the road, but if there was a storm in the air he would run like a frightened rabbit. I wasn't much for horses and he seemed to know it. Sometimes I would forget that he had a stomach and if it wasn't for Mirandy reminding me he would have gone without his dinner many times. I wasn't very good about keeping his stall clean either. One day one of the farmers went into the barn and found the poor horse standing with his back legs about two feet higher than his front legs. The farmer shook his head.

"Mr. Joshua," he said. "You must clean that horse's stall. He will

never stay healthy this way." Well, the farmer found my shovel and he cleaned it out for me.

"There," he said. "You teach the children, but it takes a farmer to teach the teacher." Believe me, I never let it happen again. From that day on the old horse lived in a clean stall.

"Did you have a garden like my pa has, Uncle Josh?" Cee-Cee asked.

"No, the farmers brought us all we needed," Uncle Josh said. "Oh, Aunt Mirandy had a few flowers but we had trouble with the wild rabbits eating the plants, so mostly we were just content with the flowers that grew along every roadside, the sunflowers. They were not great big ones, but more like large daisies. Kansas is called the sunflower state, you know. Mirandy used to go out and pick big bouquets of them and put them in a vase on the kitchen table. We thought they were real pretty, but the farmers didn't pay any attention to them. For them the sunflowers were just a part of Kansas."

"Did they have telephones in Kansas?" Martha asked.

"Oh, yes, we had telephones all right," Uncle Josh said and he smiled.

If you had something you wanted to keep a secret you never told it on the telephone. Aunt Mirandy found that out almost as soon as we moved there. You see, we all had party lines and if I was talking on the phone to someone, anybody could pick up their phone and listen to what I was saying. And if someone would call our house and I would answer, I could hear the click of all the phones in the whole countryside as the farmer's wives took them off the hook. It happened one day that Aunt Mirandy was visiting a neighbor lady when someone rang our number—two long rings and two short rings. Those rings sounded not only in our house, but in everyone else's too. "Quick, Lena," the lady said to her little girl. "Listen in. That's the teacher's ring."

"Oh, but you must not do that," Aunt Mirandy said.

But the lady was not ashamed. "Why, that's one of the reasons we have a telephone," she said. "That's the way we hear all the news."

So we learned fast that no reports about any of the children could ever be told on the telephone.

"Well, I guess that's enough of the stories about Kansas," Uncle Josh said. "I think Aunt Mirandy has your hot chocolate ready. I can smell it. And today is sugar cookie day. But, first to the pump, everybody. Wash your hands and use the soap. Sugar cookies, hot chocolate, and clean hands all go together."

2
Caring

A warm summer rain was falling and it was Saturday morning. Uncle Josh waited on the porch. He knew the children would be coming soon.

"Mirandy," he called. "Just come and look."

Aunt Mirandy joined him on the porch. "Look at what?" she said.

Uncle Josh pointed down the hill. "Look at the children," he said. "The big ones are half way over here but poor little Lulu is way behind them."

Uncle Josh and Aunt Mirandy waited on the porch and when the older ones arrived Uncle Josh said, "What's the big hurry? Look around. You left Lulu all by herself. Poor little caboose. Cee-Cee, why didn't you help her? She's your sister."

"Oh, Pa says she helps herself real good," Cee-Cee said.

"Did your pa say that you should never help her?" Uncle Josh wanted to know.

"No, Pa didn't say that," Cee-Cee said.

"Well, I think it would be nice if you would run back and take her hand."

Cee-Cee ran back and when she finally brought Lulu to the porch Uncle Josh picked her up and held her on his lap. There were no tears in her eyes, but some dirty smudges on her cheeks told Uncle Josh that she had cried a little.

"Now, now," he said as he rubbed her little legs. "They have a lot of growing to do. Cee-Cee, come here a minute." Cee-Cee came and Uncle Josh set Lulu down beside her. "Just look at that now," he said. "Her little legs are only half as long as yours, Cee-Cee. Now, you take one great big giant step and hold it there." Cee-Cee took her step. "Now, Lulu," Uncle Josh said. "One big giant step." Lulu stretched one little leg as far

as she could. "You see, it's the same thing," Uncle Josh said. "It reaches only half as far as yours, Cee-Cee." He picked Lulu up again. "Come on, all of you: David, Martha, Seth, Cee-Cee. We'll go in the kitchen today. It's damp and chilly out here. And besides, Aunt Mirandy is making fried cakes and they really smell good."

"Oh, Uncle Josh," David said. "You have a new round rug on the floor."

"That we have," Uncle Josh said. "Mirandy and I bought it especially for the five of you. We'll call it the listening rug. Try it out. Do you like it?"

"It's soft," Lulu said, as she dug her little fingers into the soft nap.

"M-m-m-m, we like it. We love it, Uncle Josh," they all said.

Miranda beamed and Uncle Josh smiled a big, broad smile. Pleasing the children brought pleasure to them too.

The children settled down, legs crossed. "What's the story about today, Uncle Josh?" Seth asked.

"Well," Uncle Josh said, and he stroked his chin. "I think I'll tell you a story about a snake. And it will be a true story. It happened in Kansas."

The children all squirmed. "Ugh," David said.

Uncle Josh began.

School was over for the year and it was a hot summer day. Aunt Mirandy and I were having coffee on our front porch with a neighbor who had happened by. People knew that there was always coffee to be had at the teacher's house—coffee and something special that Aunt Mirandy had baked. Today it was a raisin coffee cake and we were busy talking and snacking when suddenly we noticed that something was moving through the grass.

"A snake, a snake," Aunt Mirandy cried.

"It's a viper," the neighbor said. "Quick, get me your shovel."

As soon as I got up to get it and there was movement on the porch, the snake raised its head and hissed at us angrily. I got the shovel and the neighbor was quick. He had killed many snakes before and he brought that shovel down hard right behind the snake's head. "There," he said "He's dead! We'll leave it right there and by tomorrow morning some animal will have carried it away." So we went on with our coffee party.

About a half an hour later Aunt Mirandy got up to get some more coffee and in the very same spot a snake raised its head and hissed loudly.

Aunt Mirandy screamed. "Look! Look!" she cried, "you didn't really kill it."

"Oh, but I did!" the neighbor said and he quickly got up to look. And what do you think! It was another snake, the mate, I guess, that had wound his body around the dead snake. You see, even though it was dead, he was still taking care of it.

"What did the neighbor do?" David asked.

"Well, he killed that one too," Uncle Josh said. "Remember, it was a poisonous snake. If it had been just a little harmless snake we would have done nothing. But we knew it was a viper. Viper is a name that is given to all poisonous snakes. So, it's best that you stay away from all of them."

When Uncle Josh had finished, Aunt Mirandy tapped a silver spoon on the plate of fried cakes. "There's the dinner bell," Uncle Josh said.

"Um-m-m. Fried cakes rolled in sugar," the children said. It wasn't long before the plate was empty and the cups were empty too.

"It's time to start for home," Uncle Josh said. And as the children left the porch and started down the hill he called after them.

"Remember, even snakes take care of each other. Don't forget that Lulu has little, short legs."

3
Moppit

Uncle Josh was busy in the tool shed and before he knew it there were voices on the front porch, voices that called, "Uncle Josh! Aunt Mirandy!"

Uncle Josh came quickly and went to the pump to wash his hands. "Good morning, good morning, little sugar plums,"

he said. "You're early today and you caught me at my work bench."

"What are you making, Uncle Josh?" David asked.

"A footstool," he said. "A footstool for Aunt Mirandy and when I get it finished I'll show it to you. See that pillow over there on the porch? Aunt Mirandy made that and it will fit on top of the stool.

Then Uncle Josh looked at Seth. "Why, Seth," he said. "What's wrong? I think I see tear smudges."

Seth put his head down and said nothing.

"His pa gave him a whippin'" Cee-Cee said.

"Never mind, Cee-Cee," Uncle Josh said. "Come on, Seth, why don't you tell me about it."

Cee-Cee's little mouth was ready to begin the story, but Uncle Josh stopped her again. "Wait a minute, wait a minute," he said. "I'd like Seth to tell me himself. Come on, Seth. What was wrong?"

Seth looked up at Uncle Josh. "I was supposed to do some

chores for Pa," he said. "But I went to David's house and then I forgot to do them."

"Then the whippin' was because you didn't obey your pa. Right, Seth?"

Seth nodded his head.

"Well, there is one big lesson we all have to learn when we are little," Uncle Josh said. "It's the lesson of obedience. Suppose we get on with our story. But say, maybe we ought to have a cookie first. I'm kind of hungry myself. Mirandy, Mirandy, may we each have one cookie?"

This was something new. A cookie before the story and a cookie after the story! Uncle Josh got big smiles from all of the children and an especially big one from Seth. Seth seemed to know that the extra cookie was a little salve for his whipping.

"What's the story going to be about today, Uncle Josh?" David asked.

Uncle Josh rolled his eyes and tapped his forehead with

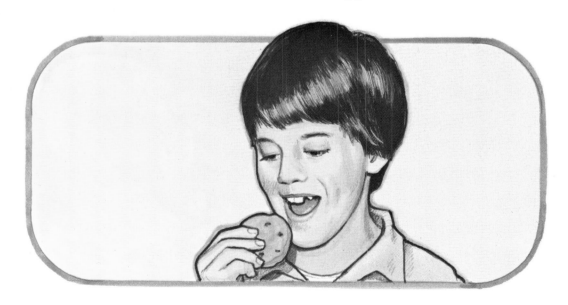

his finger. "Well, now, let's see," he said. "I think I will tell you a dog story. Do you like stories about dogs?"

"Oh, yes, yes," the children said.

Now, this is a true story. I mean that it really happened. You see, where we lived in Kansas, it was out in the farm land. Our little house was next to the school and next to the school there was a church and beyond the church was the house where the preacher lived.

Well, that preacher and his wife had a little dog, a poodle that they had brought with them from their home in the city. And it was a special dog. Oh, it didn't look like the poodles you see pictures of today, all clipped and fancied up with painted toenails and hair ribbons, looking ready for a dog party. He was just a plain poodle

with shaggy legs and uncut hair hanging over his eyes. His head looked just like Mirandy's cleaning mop and that is exactly what they called him—Moppit. No, there was nothing special about his looks, but he was a special dog just the same. Special, because he had been a show dog. You see, the preacher's wife had a brother who was a doctor, and the dog belonged to one of his patients. But the patient became very sick and had no family, so she asked the doctor if he would take her dog. It looked as though she was not going to get well and she would not be able to take care of it. The doctor agreed, but when he brought the dog home his cranky wife wanted no part of it.

"Give it away," she said. "A dog is something I don't need. Give it to your sister Kate. She loves all kinds of animals."

And so Kate, the preacher's wife, got the dog. I told you before that he had been a show dog. He could do all of the tricks some other dogs do, like rolling over, jumping through a hoop, playing dead and begging. But he could also dance to music. When Kate would sit down at the piano and say, "Dance, Moppit, dance," the dog would get up on his hind legs and dance along with the music. "Dance around the table," Kate would say, and around the table he

would go. He would keep on dancing until the music stopped. Then in a second he would be on the piano bench next to Kate, waiting for his usual piece of peppermint. That was always a reward for his performance. But, you see, there was a very important thing that little dog had learned, and that was to be obedient. He had learned, not only all of the tricks, but to obey the people who owned him and to do exactly what they said.

32

Then one day a strange thing happened. It was a hot Sunday in the middle of the summer and at exactly five minutes to ten the bell in the belfry of the country church began to ring, telling all farmers that they had five more minutes to get to church.

The minister, who always had trouble getting to church and to meetings on time, came running from the house, his sermon in his hand. Kate followed him to the screen door, but she forgot to lock it. There was to be no church service for her that morning because a new baby had arrived at the parsonage just a week before.

The minister took his place on the platform behind the pulpit and the service began. The singing was not as good as usual. It was too hot. The windows were all open and the hot Kansas sand blew against the screens. Usually the church doors were kept closed during the service, but that day they were flung wide open to let every possible breeze into the church. As the service went on, the children, sitting snugly next to their mothers, began to wiggle and to squirm. The women kept their fans moving back and forth at a fast pace and everyone hoped the sermon would be short.

But suddenly a stranger walked in at the open front door. At least, he was a stranger to the churchgoers. On soft feet he came in, holding his head high and proudly he walked down the aisle, straight to the platform. It was Moppit. Quickly he climbed the steps to the

pulpit and looked pleadingly up at his master, the minister. The minister's face reddened and he wiped his forehead with his hand-kerchief. He went on with his sermon but the people could see that he was excited.

The children began to giggle and the grown-ups snickered, while no one listened to the sermon. Finally the chief elder got up from his seat in the middle of the church and went to the platform. He wanted to pick up that little rascal and bring him back outdoors. But when he reached for Moppit the little dog quickly got up and

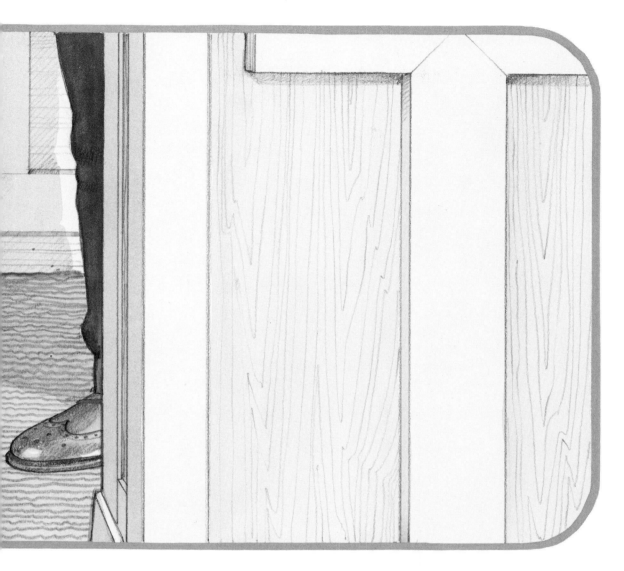

went to the other side of the minister. The elder followed and Moppit went back to the other side, and for a little while the game of tag went on, the dog moving back and forth from one side to the other and the elder following. At last the minister stopped preaching, pointed to his little pet, and said in a strong voice, "MOPPIT, YOU GO HOME." Well, that little dog obeyed on the spot. Putting his tail between his legs, he walked down the steps of the platform and then down the aisle and out of the front door. You see, he had learned to obey when he was a puppy.

"What did the minister say to Kate for not locking the screen door?" David asked.

"I don't know. I wasn't there," Uncle Josh said. "But Moppit never went to church again, so I suppose Kate was more careful."

"What happened to Moppit after that?" Cee-Cee asked.

"Well, he lived several more years, but you know he was not a young dog when Kate got him. After a few more years he got sick, and, well, I guess he went to the place that the Indians call the happy hunting grounds. But where he went doesn't matter. What does matter is that the people always remembered him as the dog who came to church and then did exactly what he was told to do."

4
The Big City

Aunt Miranda had become just as attached to the children as Uncle Josh. She was always trying to think of different ways to please them and today she had a very special idea. The apples on the apple tree were ripe and beautiful. Spraying that tree was one job that Uncle Josh never forgot. He wanted no wormy apples.

"But do you think an apple is such a treat for a child?" Uncle Josh said. "I think they have apple trees of their own."

"It won't be just an apple," Aunt Miranda answered. "It will be a dressed apple."

"What in the world is a dressed apple?" Uncle Josh asked.

"It's an apple that is dressed in a caramel coat," Aunt Miranda said as she smiled.

"Well, how about that!" Uncle Josh exclaimed. "But when do you expect to get them ready? It's almost time for the children to come."

"I made the caramel yesterday and it will need only a little heating," Aunt Mirandy said, "and as for the rest, the children will dress their own apples. It will be more fun that way. See, I have the sticks laid out and the waxed paper is ready for the cooling."

"Where are the apples?" Uncle Josh asked.

"On the tree," Aunt Mirandy said. "With a little help from us I thought it would be nice for the children to pick their own."

The children certainly did enjoy picking their own. Uncle Josh did not have to urge them to pick big ones. They all had eyes for the biggest apple on the tree, but they needed a little boosting from Uncle Josh to reach the apple they wanted.

"Now wash the apples at the pump," Aunt Mirandy said, "and then take them to the kitchen. And wash your hands too."

Aunt Mirandy had put the caramel on a slow fire and

when the children entered the kitchen there were squeals of delight."

"Oh, it smells wonderful in here! It smells so good! It smells like a candy store!" they shouted.

Uncle Josh pushed the sticks well into the apples so they would be very tight and the fun began.

"All right," Uncle Josh said, "the oldest first."

David stepped up.

"Dip it way into the caramel," Aunt Mirandy said. "Now twist it a little so it's well covered. That's right. Now take it out, let it drip off a little into the pan, and set it on the waxed paper."

Seth came next, then Cee-Cee, then Martha and last of all

little Lulu. She was almost ready for her fourth birthday now. Lulu needed a little help and as she stood on a kitchen chair, Aunt Mirandy held her hand and dipped along with her.

"I can do it all by myself," Lulu said.

"Oh, I know," Aunt Mirandy told her. "But if I help you just a little bit your apple will have a thicker coat and it will taste much better."

When everyone had finished, Aunt Mirandy said, "Now we will let them cool while Uncle Josh tells you a story and then you can eat them on the way home."

"All right," Uncle Josh called. "Sit down! I was really going to tell you an animal story, but the caramel apples reminded me of something I did when I was as old as David and I think you'd like to hear about it."

I had an aunt and an uncle and a cousin Ellen who lived in Chicago and I lived here in Kentucky, but not in this house. We often had letters from my aunt and one day a very special letter came. Inside of it was a picture of Ellen. She was sitting in a goat wagon and hitched to the wagon was the prettiest little goat you ever did see. My mother thought I would be so pleased to look at it, but I wasn't.

"Put it away!" I said. "I don't want to look at it!"

"Why not?" my mother asked.

"Because I don't like it," I said.

Now, maybe you can guess why I was so naughty and so mean about it. Don't you see, I was jealous—jealous that Ellen had a goat

and I didn't. I think my mother understood, though, because she put the picture away and for a long, long time I didn't see it again.

And then one day we got another letter from auntie inviting my mother and me to come for a visit. Oh, what fun! I had never had a train ride and what a big day that was. We ate in the dining car and sat for a long time in the observation car which was the last car on the long train.

My aunt and uncle and Ellen met us in the depot and the very first thing I said to Ellen was, "Say, do you still have that goat?"

Imagine how surprised and sad I was when she said, "A goat? A goat? I never had a goat."

"The picture, the picture," I said. "You were sitting in the goat wagon."

Everyone laughed and I didn't know why. Finally my aunt said, "That wasn't Ellen's goat, Joshua. There was a man who came through the neighborhood with his goat wagon. He wanted to take pictures of children and he took Ellen's picture."

Well, then I was really sad. You see, even though I was jealous of Ellen because she had a goat and I didn't, I was looking forward to driving that goat.

Believe me, life was different in Chicago than it was here in a tiny town in Kentucky. There were so many different things to see.

In Kentucky we didn't know what an alley was, but Chicago was full of alleys. The side of Ellen's house was right on an alley and every day the rats would play there. About every hour a rag man would come through. Each rag man had his own way of calling and some of them even put their calls to a tune. People who lived there

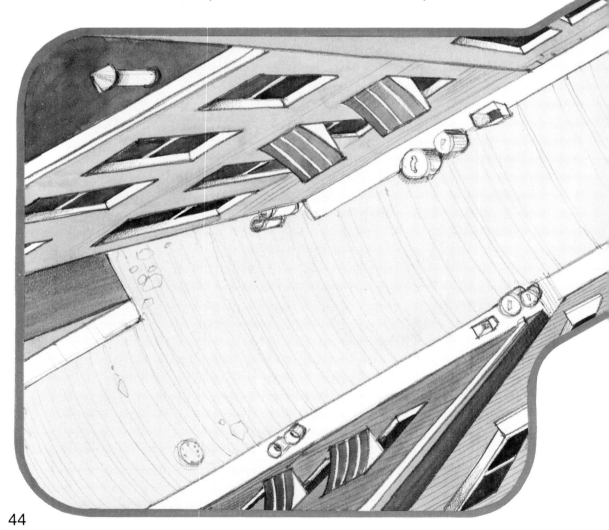

knew exactly which one was coming by the call he gave. One would simply shout, "Rags! . . . Rags! . . . Rags!" Another made a little tune and sang, "Rags an' ole' iron, Rags an' ole' iron." Still another would call in a big deep voice, "Old rags, Old rags," and then to his horse he would say, "Giddap, giddap, giddap." So every time he hollered "Rags," his horse would be told to "giddap."

"What do they really want?" I asked my uncle one day.

"Exactly what they say," he said. "They want to buy our old rags, newspapers, and iron and then they sell them again for more money than they paid us. Listen! Here comes the one who sings, 'Rags an' ole' iron.' We never sell to him because he cheats the people. He puts his fingers under the scale to raise it so things don't show as much on the scale as they really weigh."

One day Ellen and I were outside climbing the tree that grew right in front of my uncle's front porch. Suddenly there was music in the air. "Listen," I said. "I hear music."

"That's the organ grinder," Ellen said. "Hurry, we have to get some pennies."

"Why?" I asked.

"Oh, you'll see," she said and she fairly flew into the house. "Some pennies, Daddy," she said. "May we have some pennies? The organ grinder is coming!"

My uncle gave us each three pennies and I thought we were going to give them to the organ grinder for playing his music. But when he came he had not only a hand organ, but also a monkey on a long leather leash. And what do you think! That monkey wore clothes. He was dressed in a bright red suit, all trimmed with gold braid and on his head he wore a flat little red hat that tied under his chin.

When they got to the corner of the alley the organ grinder stopped and other children came running from the surrounding houses. When he thought the crowd was big enough he began to play. When the music started the monkey began to dance and do little tricks. He somersaulted, turned hand-springs, rolled over and over, and made funny faces. When the monkey finished his tricks the music stopped. The monkey untied the string under his chin, took off his little hat, and using it for a collection plate, went around to all the children to collect their pennies. Each penny went from his hat into a pocket on his jacket, and when the pocket was full he went to his master who took the pennies out and put them in his own pocket.

I thought that monkey was the nicest thing that I had ever seen. For many years after that I wished I could have one for a pet, especially one who would collect pennies for me.

There were other things in Chicago that I had never known about. One day Ellen asked her mother if we could each have a nickel so we could go to the corner grocery store. Oh, that store was something wonderful! The long penny-candy case was full of different kinds of candy. It reached from the front to the back of the store. But Ellen wasn't after candy. I followed her to a big barrel.

"I'm going to get a dill pickle," she said. "Look!" Using the scoop on the side of the barrel, she fished out a great big dill pickle.

"Oh, I want one too," I said. And that's where our nickels went.

On another day as we played outside, there was a sudden whistling noise in the air, the same kind of noise that your mother's whistling tea kettle makes, only much louder.

Ellen made another trip into the house, bounding up the porch steps as fast as she could go. By the time she came out the whistling was in front of the house. The driver stopped his horse.

"What is it? What is it?" I cried.

"It's the waffle man," Ellen said. "Come on."

The whistling stopped. The wagon had glass all around it and there were waffles on one side and carameled apples on the other side, only they were called taffy apples.

"Let's get a waffle today and the next time he comes we'll get a taffy apple," Ellen said.

The waffles were big and square and good; they were crisp like a cookie and sprinkled all over the top with powdered sugar. No wonder the children loved the waffle man.

By this time David and the other children were turning their heads. When Uncle Josh talked about taffy apples it reminded them of their own carameled apples.

Uncle Josh saw that. "Story time is over," he said.

The children were on their feet in a hurry, each taking the carameled apple they had made, and each saying a thank you to Aunt Mirandy.

Uncle Josh smiled as he watched them go down the hill munching their goodies. "You know the old saying, Mirandy," he said. "'An apple a day keeps the doctor away,'" and then he added, "but with a taffy apple a day, there's the dentist to pay."

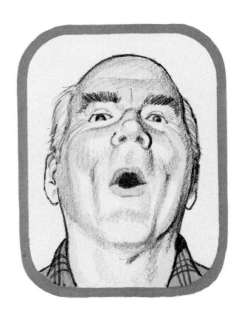

5

Polly

Uncle Josh sat on the porch waiting for the first sight of the children on the hillside. Aunt Miranda sat beside him.

"What do you have for a treat for them today?" Uncle Josh asked.

"Something I have never made before," she said. "Do you remember the last time that they were here and you told them the story of the waffle man?"

"I sure do," Uncle Josh said.

"Well, I experimented a little yesterday when you were down in the valley," Aunt Miranda said, "and I found out that I make a pretty good waffle man. I took our old waffle iron out of the cupboard and made some just exactly like I always did for our breakfast. And then, when they were done, I put them in the oven until they were cookie-crisp and I sprinkled them with powdered sugar. And do you know what, Joshua, I ate them all for my lunch. So today while you are telling your story I will be making waffles. The children ought to like that."

Suddenly Uncle Josh put his hand on his forehead and peered down the hillside.

"Now just look, Mirandy," he said. "There's a war going on down there. It looks like David and Seth are in trouble."

"Oh, my," Aunt Miranda said. "Joshua, maybe you should run down there."

"No, no," Uncle Josh said. "I'm getting too old to run down that hill. David and Seth will have to fight their own battle. Besides, I think the war has almost come to an end. Look! They're on the way up here."

Both David and Seth looked ashamed when they reached the porch. Seth had a bloody nose. He had been wiping it on his sleeve and that didn't make him look very nice.

"I see you had a problem," Uncle Josh said. "Who wants to tell me about it?"

Cee-Cee was the most eager. "Seth and David had a fight," she said.

"That I can see," Uncle Josh said. "David, suppose you tell me about it."

David looked down. "I did it," he said.

"The question is WHY," Uncle Josh said. "You know, there's a reason for everything under the sun. Why did you do it?"

"Because Seth always teases me," he said. "Over and over he tells me I'm too fat and he calls me names."

"Well, now we have the answer," Uncle Josh said, and turning to Seth he asked, "Is that true?"

Now Seth hung his head. "Yes, sir," he said.

"Usually," Uncle Josh said, "it's the one who does the punching who gets the blame, but the fault really lies with the teaser. I remember when I was a growing boy my mother used to say, 'You can tease an animal until he bites,' and I guess that goes for children too. And, Seth, name calling is cheap, very cheap. Will you remember that?"

"Yes, sir," he said again.

Aunt Miranda took Seth inside and washed away the bloody streaks. The fight seemed forgotten.

But Uncle Josh had not forgotten. He knew just the story he had tucked away in his mind and he thought it would fit the day. When everyone was seated and quiet he began.

"Do you remember the story I told you about Moppit, the dog who went to church?" he asked.

The children giggled. "Oh, yes!" they said.

"And do you remember that I told you about Kate, the minister's wife, who owned Moppit?"

"Yes, yes," the children said.

Well, today's story is about Kate and a bird she owned before she came to Kansas to live. She didn't take it along, however, because it was such a noisy little fellow that she was glad to leave him behind and have her parents take care of it.

The bird was a parrot and they called her Polly. Having a parrot was quite the style in those days and there were many of them around. Kate always said she never came across one that could talk like Polly. In fact, I once heard her say, "I believe that bird could not only talk, but it seemed that she could think."

She was never in a cage, but always sat on a perch in the dining room. That was the main room in their house. No meals were ever served in the kitchen, but always in the dining room. The room also had some comfortable chairs and rockers. It was Polly's home too, the most lived-in room in the house.

Polly knew every one of the family members by name, Mama, Papa, Edward, Robert and Kate. She never got them mixed up. Whenever anyone came home Polly would always greet them. If it was Robert she would always say, "Hello, Rob," never "Hello, Ed." But her first love was for Kate. Kate was the one who talked to her, fed her little sweetmeats, and cleaned the box under her perch.

Often Polly was a nuisance. Edward took piano lessons and his teacher said he should count every note he played, which he tried to do—one and two and, one and two and. Then Polly would shriek, "One and two and, one and two and," until Edward couldn't stand it. He would call, "Mama, put that bird in the kitchen. She mocks every-thing I say and she gets me all mixed up." So Polly would be stuck in a corner of the kitchen. "No, Ma, no, Ma," the bird would say. She loved the dining room and couldn't stand being alone in the kitchen.

Mealtimes for the family were the noisiest time of all. The father opened the meals with a prayer and Polly would mimic every word he said. After the father said "Amen," Polly would say, "Amen, Squawk!" The boys would giggle. Father finally said, "All right, after

this the bird must go in the closet during mealtime." That didn't make matters much better, for as soon as the door was closed, Polly would say in pleading squawks, "It's dark in here, it's dark in here. Polly doesn't like it." She would repeat it over and over until the door was finally opened.

Polly was also a tattletale. She saw everything that went on and she reported it all to the mother. It was Kate's job to prepare the evening meal while mother mended in the dining room. But Kate had a habit of tasting little bits of food from the various cooking pots. She was busy doing this one day when her mother called, "Kate, I know just what you're doing. You're sampling the food."

"How do you know?" Kate called.

"Listen to the bird," her mother said.

Kate listened, and Polly was saying, "M-m-m-m. Like it, Kate? Polly likes some too."

"Pesky bird," Kate said to herself, but she got wise to Polly. Whenever she felt like tasting the food she gave Polly some first and then the bird would be quiet.

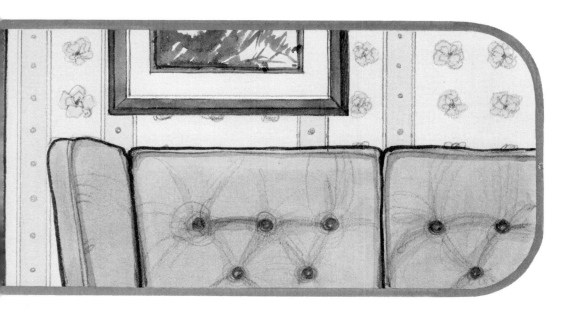

There wasn't much that anyone could do to make that old bird angry, but there was one way that Kate knew to tease her. Kate had long hair which she combed up and rolled on the top of her head. She pinned it down with hair pins and when she wanted to recomb it she often let Polly take out the hair pins. She would come close to Polly's perch and begin scratching her body softly. One by one Polly would take out the pins and put them in Kate's free hand. Starting near her feet, Kate would scratch, moving her hand gradually toward the top of Polly's body. When Kate thought the last pin had come out she would suddenly come close to her ear, which Polly didn't like. With her sharp beak Polly would make a dive to peck her hand, but Kate would always pull it away just in time.

"You're going to tease her once too often," her mother would say, "and then you'll be sorry." And that is just what happened. Kate pulled her hand back quickly, just as she always did, but Polly was too fast. Polly caught Kate's finger and bit down hard. The blood spurted out.

"You're a naughty bird, Polly,"
Kate said.

"You're a very naughty bird."

"Oh, no,"
Kate's mother said.

"You're the naughty one.
You teased her just long enough
    until she bit you.
Now go and soak your finger
    in peroxide."

Aunt Mirandy thought the children had heard enough about Polly and she blew a little whistle. "The waffle man is here," she called.

Out of the oven came the waffles and as Uncle Josh bit into one, he said, "Mirandy, Mirandy, it's just like Chicago."

The children got a waffle in each hand and Uncle Josh started them on their way home.

David turned around. "What finally happened to Polly, Uncle Josh?"

"Oh," Uncle Josh said. "Well, one day Kate got a letter from her father and at the end of the letter he wrote:

> I am so very sad to say,
> Our dear old Polly died today.
> And I feel bad, but not the boys,
> They say, "Hurray, we'll have less noise."

6
Shadow

U ncle Josh and Aunt Miranda had settled down in a comfortable chair, looking forward to a quiet evening.

Suddenly there was a noise on the front porch. "Meow!"

Aunt Miranda looked at Uncle Josh. "There's a cat out there." And then they heard it again. "Meow!"

Aunt Miranda was on her feet in a hurry. She opened the

front door and there, sitting and looking pleadingly up at her, was a big black cat.

"Well, come in Mrs. Black," she said.

The cat walked in as though the cabin had always been her home.

"She's hungry," Aunt Miranda said.

Uncle Josh warned her. "Remember, Mirandy, when you once feed a stray cat, she's your cat forever."

"I know, I know," Mirandy said, "but she looks thin and hungry." Mirandy opened the refrigerator and found a little of this and a little of that and altogether it made a good cat dinner. She filled another bowl with milk and the cat had a feast. When Mrs. Black had finished eating, her little paw became her wash cloth and she scrubbed her face clean. Then she looked around and laid herself down at Aunt Miranda's feet.

"I told you," Uncle Josh said. "You got yourself a cat."

"That's fine with me," Aunt Mirandy said. "It's lonesome up here when you go down into the valley and the cat will be company for me."

As the days went by Mrs. Black made herself more and more at home. Aunt Mirandy put a warm, woolly blanket in one corner of the kitchen, and that was a haven for the cat.

Nevertheless, Uncle Josh and Aunt Mirandy were not at all ready for the surprise Mrs. Black gave them. When Uncle Josh went into the kitchen one morning, lo and behold! Snuggled next to Mrs. Black were two tiny kittens, one gray one and one black one.

Uncle Josh went back to the bedroom to find Aunt Miranda. He threw up his hands. "Mirandy," he said. "Mrs. Black sure knows her arithmetic. She knows how to multiply. We no longer have one cat. We have three!"

Aunt Miranda ran into the kitchen. "Oh, my! One cat, yes, but three is a no-no. But never mind, Joshua, we'll find homes for them somewhere when they're ready to leave Mrs. Black."

When the children came for their next visit they were delighted to find the kittens. Martha, who was always the quiet one, was full of smiles and tiny squeals. She petted the tiny black kitten and let his scrawny little tail curl around her finger. "Look, Aunt Mirandy," she said. "He has a tail like a licorice stick."

Aunt Mirandy laughed. "You're right, Martha," she said. I think that maybe you have given that black kitten a name. We'll call it Licorice. It's a real sugar name." That pleased Martha and she looked longingly at the little bundle of black fur.

When the children had seen enough of the kittens, Uncle Josh told them to find their places. "I'm going to tell you a story about a little girl in Kansas and about the cat who went to school."

Maria was a sad little girl but we never knew why. She had a good home, a nice mother and father, but she had no brothers or sisters.

Then it happened one day that Maria came in from the recess playtime and she brought a kitten into the schoolroom with her. She hugged it closely, and when I asked her where she found the cat, she said, "He's my cat. He follows me wherever I go." Well, it was true that he had been following her around the playground.

"What are you going to do about him?" I asked.

Maria answered, "He could sleep in the play corner."

We had a few old toys which some of the mothers had brought to school for the very little children to play with on rainy days. Included in the toys was a doll bed complete with an old doll and some blankets.

"All right," I said to Maria. "You try the kitten in the play corner." Well, it quickly adopted that corner and hopped into the doll bed. That was the first time that I saw Maria really laugh and be happy.

When school was over for the day Maria carried the kitten home. The next morning the kitten followed her into the schoolroom and went straight to the doll bed. It was as though he was telling us, "I know I have to be quiet here, so I'll just go to sleep."

This went on for quite some time and when people would ask me how many pupils I had in school I got to saying, "Thirty-five and one cat."

Then came the day when the children had a day off from school so that I could have a visit with each of the parents.

When Maria's folks came, I said, "Well, we had better talk about both of your family members, Maria and her cat."

Her mother looked at me and said, "Oh, but it's not her cat. We have never had a cat. When Maria is home she calls it the school cat. It follows Maria wherever she goes, so her father and I call it her shadow. And now we have been calling the cat by that name—Shadow."

This was news to me. Then we talked about how much happier Maria was since the kitten had come into her life. Her mother said that they had noticed a big difference too and so we agreed to go on just the way we had been doing. But we also decided that Maria must know Shadow was really to be her cat and that no one would take him away from her.

From that time on Maria was a different child. Shadow was with her all the time, following her to school, following her home, sleeping at the foot of her bed each night and lying close to her at mealtime. He was a cat that needed a special friend and Maria was a little girl who needed a special love. And she found her love in that cat.

Uncle Josh noticed how interested Martha was in the story and after the children had eaten their snacks and were on their way home, he said, "You know, Mirandy, Martha could be a second Maria. Maybe that little black kitten of ours, which she named Licorice, should belong to her."

"Wait a minute, Joshua," Miranda said. "Maybe her mother wouldn't agree with you. We can't just hand Martha a cat and say, Here, take it home."

"No, I wouldn't do that," Uncle Josh said. "One of these days I'll go and see her mother and we'll have a little talk."

That time came soon. Uncle Josh picked a day when it was sunny. Sunshine warms the hearts of people. He also picked a time when he knew Martha would be in school. Then, if her mother's answer was no, Martha would never know about it.

A light knock on the door brought Martha's mother to open it. "Why Mr. Joshua," she said. "Come in, and what brings you here on this beautiful day?"

"Martha," Uncle Josh said.

"Martha?" her mother said. "What has she done?"

"Oh, nothing. Nothing bad," he said. "It's just that she doesn't seem like a very happy little girl and I worry a bit about her."

"You're right," Martha's mother said. "Oh, I don't think she's terribly unhappy, but she certainly is not a smiling, outgoing little girl."

"May I tell you a story?" Uncle Josh asked. "It's a story I told the children the last time they came to visit."

"I would like to hear one of your stories," Martha's mother said. "The children are always talking about your stories and they try to retell them but I'm sure they miss a lot."

And then Uncle Josh told her the story of Maria and the cat who went to school. He ended by telling her how Martha had given their little black kitten the name of Licorice. "And now I think," he said, "that if you would allow Miranda and me to give the little black kitten to Martha it might do for her what the stray cat did for Maria."

Martha's mother thought for a minute and then she said, "I'm not really a lover of cats, Mr. Joshua, but if you think it would please Martha we'll try it."

Uncle Josh was happy. "Please don't tell her," he said. "I'll be around with the kitten some evening when I am sure that she is ready to leave the mother cat."

That time came a few weeks later. "I'm going to bring the black kitten away tonight," Uncle Josh said to Aunt Miranda.

"And I'm going with you," Aunt Miranda said. "Look on the top of the refrigerator." There stood a basket lined with a little quilt that Aunt Miranda had made. "We will leave the basket," she said. "The kitten must have a home of her own."

Together, hand in hand, Uncle Josh and Aunt Miranda walked slowly down the long hill. Once in a while there was a soft meow from the basket on Aunt Miranda's arm. It was a long walk and they were tired.

When they reached the little village in the valley, Aunt Miranda said, "I'm glad Martha's house is the first one we come to." Martha's mother answered their knock on the door. She smiled when she saw the basket. "Martha is in the kitchen," she said. "Come in quietly and sit down. We'll surprise her."

Uncle Josh and Aunt Miranda did as she had said and when they were both seated, the mother called, "Martha, Martha, come in here for a minute."

When Martha saw Uncle Josh she ran to him, gave one long leap and jumped on his lap. She looked over at Aunt Miranda and suddenly spied the basket on the floor. Almost at the same time there was a very faint meow from under the blanket.

Martha was on her feet and then on her knees beside the basket. She looked up at Aunt Miranda. "Where are you bringing Licorice?" she asked sadly.

"Well, we didn't think Mrs. Black needed her any more so we are looking for a new mother. Would you like to be that mother?"

Everyone expected Martha to be jubilant, to dance and hop and skip. But she didn't. She cried. The tears rolled down her little cheeks and dropped on the cat's fur, making little wet patches. But everyone in the room knew that the falling tears were tears of happiness and the smiles that followed the tears were like sunbeams peeking through the rain.

On the very next storytelling day Martha arrived with the empty basket.

"What now?" Aunt Mirandy asked. "That was a bed for Licorice."

"She doesn't need it." Martha said. "During the daytime she sleeps on the davenport and at night she sleeps on my bed."

"Then she doesn't need it at all," Aunt Mirandy said. "Now I know your kitten has a good home."

Aunt Mirandy felt a little tug on her skirt. It was David. Looking up at her, he asked, "Aunt Mirandy, may I have the other kitten?"

"What would your mother say?" Aunt Mirandy asked.

"She already said I could have it if you would give it to me," he answered.

Uncle Josh interrupted. "That's fine, David," he said, "but no kitten leaves this house without a name. You will have to give it a name first."

"Oh, I've already named it," David said. "I'm going to call it Kit."

"All right, David," Uncle Josh said. "He's your cat!"

7
Friends

It was an early summer morning—just the kind of a day that makes a person glad to be alive and in Kentucky. School was over for the year and Uncle Josh sat on the porch watching for the children to come.

He called to Aunt Miranda. "They're on the way, but something is wrong. I can count only four. Somebody is missing. Take a look, Mirandy. Your eyes are better than mine."

Aunt Miranda came out on the porch and watched with him. "It's one of the boys," she said finally, and when the children came closer she said, "It's Seth, and just look at David's face. He looks as though he hasn't a friend in the whole world."

When the children came up to the porch and after all the hellos were said, Uncle Josh said, "Lulu, can you count? Tell me how many children are here today." Lulu counted. "One, two, three, four," she said. "Good!" Uncle Josh said. "We used to have five, so that means that five children, take away one child, leaves how many children?" "Four," Lulu said. "That's right again," Uncle Josh said, and then, turning to David he asked, "Where's Seth?"

"He's gone on a vacation," David said sadly.

"Oh, I see," Uncle Josh said, "and, David, you're lonesome for him. Am I right?"

"Yes, he's my best friend and I don't have anyone to play with now."

"Well," Uncle Josh said. "I used to tell my school children, 'Lonesome is what lonesome does.' That means that if you sit around and do nothing but tell yourself how lonesome you are, you don't help yourself at all. You've got to find something new to do and then the time goes fast. But come on now, sit down and I'll tell you a story. I know a story, David, about a boy who had the same problem you have, and I'll tell you what he did about it."

Teddy and Tom were the same age, lived on farms next to one another, and always played together. But Tom's daddy and mother took him on a long vacation and, just like you, David, Teddy was lonesome. His mother knew he needed a friend, but there was no one. One morning, as she watched a squirrel dart from the front yard tree, she said, "Teddy, try to make friends with our farmyard squirrels." She was eager for Teddy to have something to do.

"How could I do that?" Teddy asked.

"First of all," his mother said, "you will have to use your ears. Squirrels have a language all of their own and you must listen how they chatter to each other. Then see if you can make a noise something like that. Do that first and then we'll talk about it again."

Teddy went outdoors. He waited a long, long time but finally he saw them. There were two squirrels. They were chasing each other up and down and down and up the big tree. He thought they were angry because their noises sounded angry. Tchk, tchk! Teddy tried, but he couldn't make a noise like that. Then Mother came out.

"Listen, Mom," he said. "I can't mimic the squirrels." Mother listened, and with a little tongue practice she could do quite well. She showed Teddy. "Look, click your tongue like this." Teddy tried again. Before they realized it the squirrels were sitting under the tree, listening.

Mother laughed. "It looks like we're playing this game together, Teddy, you and I. You sit right here," she said, "and I'll get some peanuts." Teddy kept clicking his tongue until Mother came back.

Giving the peanuts to Teddy, she said, "Here, throw them each one peanut. See how close you can get." Teddy threw. The squirrels caught on and Teddy had begun to make friends.

"Now," Mother said. "Every morning we'll put a few peanuts on

the porch and you watch for the squirrels. But don't get too close. Squirrels bite sometimes."

Each morning after that Teddy ate his breakfast in front of the window overlooking the porch and every morning the squirrels were there. But one morning Teddy got very excited.

"Mother! Mother," he called. "The blue jays are stealing the squirrel's peanuts."

"Well," Mother said. "It looks like we have thieves on the door-step, but the blue jays can be your friends too. Never mind, we'll put some more out there for the squirrels."

Teddy was surprised how greedy the blue jays were. They were not content with one peanut, but often took two in their beak and flew into the tree with their prize, where they would hold the peanuts down with their claws and crack them open with their long beak.

Soon Teddy noticed that when he put the peanuts out in the morning and called the squirrels with his clicking tongue, the blue jays would be the first ones there, waiting in the tree. And if Teddy would walk with his peanut bag to the back porch the blue jays would follow him. Yes, Teddy had made more friends.

Early one evening there was a very bad storm. The lightning flashed and the thunder was so loud that Teddy covered his ears. Suddenly there was a crash. Father looked out of the window. "Oh, oh," he said. "It's the tree behind the barn. It's down on the ground."

Teddy was worried. "Maybe the squirrels had a nest in that tree," he said, but his mother said, "Don't worry about it. Squirrels can take care of themselves. They're used to all kinds of weather."

The very next morning Teddy's father came into the house from the barn. He seemed excited. "Teddy," He called. "Come with me to the barn. There's something I want to show you." Together they ran to the barn. "Look in that big box," Father said.

What Teddy saw made him jump back a few steps. "Raccoons!" he shouted. "Three raccoons! A mother and two little ones!"

"Remember," Father called. "Raccoons are wild animals and they can bite." He joined Teddy beside the box.

"Where did they come from?" Teddy asked.

"I don't know for sure," Father said, "but I have an idea that they had a den in the big tree that came down last night. When their

home blew down the mother wanted to get her babies out of the rain so she carried them in here, or maybe they followed her. They are not newly born. See! Their eyes are open."

"Can we feed them?" Teddy asked.

"Yes," Father said. "They'll eat bread, and then Teddy noticed that Father had already put a pan of water beside the box. "Coons like their food wet," he said.

Teddy smiled. "I have some more friends," he said. What wonderful friends they turned out to be. They seemed altogether unafraid of Teddy and followed him around the farm. He watched them as the mother dug under old logs for crickets and grubs and taught her children how to do it. He watched again as the mother waded at the edge of the creek, pulling out crabs and clams. She showed her little ones where to find acorns and how to crack the shells. They learned quickly not to be afraid of Teddy and Teddy learned all the habits of the raccoons. He spent so much time with them that his mother had to remind him to pay a little attention to the squirrels and the blue jays.

The time passed quickly for him. Each day he learned a little more about the habits of his friends; how the squirrels became angry and clawed at the screen door when the peanuts were gone; how the blue jays became noisy and scolded if the treats were gone;

and how they flew at the squirrels, making them scatter when the jays wanted the food.

There came a day when Teddy slept longer than usual and Mother put out the food for the animals. When he finally came down Mother had his breakfast ready and when he sat down to eat Mother looked out of the window.

"Oh, my," she said. "Oh, my! We have another thief on the door-step! He's eating your peanuts! It's a boy!"

Teddy jumped up. "Tom!" he cried. "Tom's home from his vacation!"

Uncle Josh looked at David. "Think about it David," he said. "There's a cure for being lonesome. And now let's see what Aunt Mirandy has for us."

And what did Aunt Mirandy have? A huge kettle full of popcorn and syrup warming on the stove.

"Wash your hands and scrub them hard," she said. When they had finished she poured the syrup over the popcorn and each child had a turn to make two popcorn balls. "One for each hand," Aunt Mirandy said. "All except David. He may make four."

"He doesn't have four hands," Cee-Cee said.

"I know that," Aunt Mirandy replied. "The extra two are for David to save for his best friend, Seth, when he comes back home.

8

Sunny

It was a beautiful summer day. Aunt Miranda and Uncle Josh had been up since early morning. For a whole week Aunt Miranda had been saving the cream that she had skimmed from the top of the milk. It had been too hot to think of making fried cakes and dipping them into the hot grease. And it was also too hot to use the oven, so that meant no cookies for the children.

"I have an idea," she had said to Uncle Josh. "Let's make ice cream. That will really please the children."

Early in the morning the ice cream freezer had come out of the far corner of the cupboard. Uncle Josh gathered all the necessities and Aunt Miranda mixed the ingredients.

"Now turn the handle," she said to Uncle Josh, as she poured all the fixings into the freezer. "While you are doing that I'll go and get some peaches from our little peach tree."

She was careful to pick only the very ripe ones. "They must be very sweet," she said to herself. "They must be sweet enough so they can do without any added sugar."

It seemed like hours to Uncle Josh that he had turned the handle of the old freezer. Aunt Miranda had finished cutting the peaches into bite sizes long ago.

"It's getting harder and harder to turn, Mirandy," he said. "You had better take a look. Maybe we have ice cream."

Aunt Miranda lifted the cover a little bit. "Well, Joshua," she said, "we have ice cream slush. Come, now, turn a few more times."

Uncle Josh turned some more until finally he said, "Mirandy, I can't turn it anymore. The handle won't move another inch. Take a look."

For the second time the cover came off. "Right you are, Joshua," Aunt Miranda said. "We have ice cream, beautiful, beautiful ice cream."

Later that morning the children arrived, puffing from their long, hot walk up the hill. They all ran to the old pump, and, taking turns, they cupped their hands together, filled them with water and splashed it over their faces, and then, cupping their hands again, they drank as much as they could.

"Come now," Uncle Josh called. "We've had enough of the cooling off."

On the porch Uncle Josh saw David sniff and sniff again.

"You sniff like a puppy dog, David," Uncle Josh said. "And I think I know why. You miss the smell of cookies and doughnuts. Right?"

David smiled a guilty smile.

"Well, don't worry about it," Uncle Josh said. "Aunt Mirandy has a special treat for you today. It's something cold, and it's a surprise. Now let's sit down. I think you're all tired."

"Uncle Josh," David said. "You often tell us about your school children. Do you and Aunt Mirandy have any children that really belong to you? Do you have any children of your own?"

Uncle Josh smiled and he scratched his head. He waited a long time before he answered David, and finally he said, "Well, yes and no."

"What does that mean?" David asked.

"Well," Uncle Josh said. "I'll tell you a story and then I'll let you answer your own question, David. How will that be?"

David thought that would be fine.

The story is about a little family who were close neighbors of ours in Kansas. It was a small family; a father and mother, a little girl named Mary and a little boy whose name was Peter. Oh, yes, and there was someone else who was almost a member of that family. It was a little black lamb that they simply called Lammy. But it was a very unusual lamb, as you will see. I guess it was because he was black. Often in a flock of newborn sheep there is one little black lamb and he is often the one who gives the shepherd the most trouble. That is why a naughty boy or girl is sometimes called the black sheep of the family. But this little lamb was different. He was special because he helped the family.

Peter and Mary's daddy was a nice man in many ways, but he had one very bad habit. About two miles away from our house, in Prairie View, there was a place where they served all kinds of liquor, and Mr. Brake liked to go there. Often he would come home very drunk. But he never went there alone. The little black lamb always trotted along with him and would wait outside for him. It got to be well known throughout the whole countryside. People would drive past the saloon in their wagons or buggies and would say, "Look, there's Lammy. Mr. Brake is in the saloon again."

This went on for a long, long time. The lamb would wait outside until Mr. Brake was ready to go home and then he would lead him all the way. But one winter day it started to snow and it turned very cold while Mr. Brake was in the saloon. A Kansas wind came up and turned the weather into a blinding storm.

Hours went by and the darkness came, but Mr. Brake did not come home. His wife was worried and even more so when the little black lamb came home all alone. She took the poor little thing into the kitchen and let him lie down beside the stove. Then she called the neighbors and the men went out in a group, all looking for Mr. Brake. But it was not until morning, when the light came, that they found his frozen body in a ditch beside the road.

Then, not quite a year later, Mrs. Brake suddenly became very sick and died. So that made quite a problem for Peter and Mary. But Mrs. Brake had a sister who lived on a nearby farm. Although she had four boys of her own she took the children to live with them, and she took the little black lamb too.

That was fine for Peter but there were too many boys for Mary, and she began coming over to our house. We had never called her Mary. In school I always said she was my little Kansas sunflower,

and somehow we started calling her Sunny. And sunny she was! She was always sweet and smiling, like a sunny summer day. The funny part of it was that when we began to call her Sunny everyone else did too and she was no longer Mary to anyone.

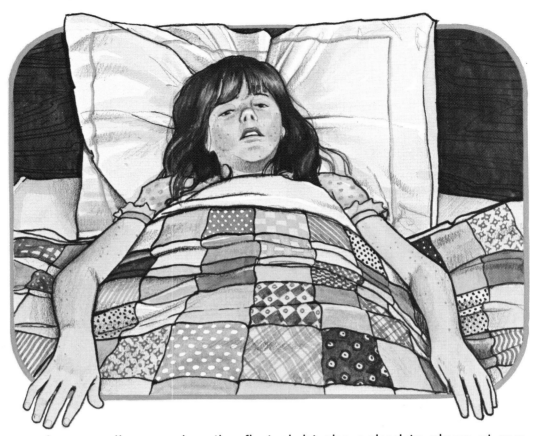

I can well remember the first night she asked to sleep at our house. "Call your auntie," Mirandy said, "and if it suits her it will suit us too." Well, her auntie didn't care and so we tucked Sunny into the big bed in the spare bedroom. But when she awoke in the morning she no longer looked like the smiling little Sunny. She was peppered with chicken pox. That meant that she was not able to go home because there were five boys there who would surely get the chicken pox. So there was nothing for us to do but to keep her with us.

Sunny was sick for several days and by the time all of the blisters were gone and she was feeling well again she didn't want to go back to her auntie's house and we didn't like to part with her. So she stayed. Auntie didn't mind. She had plenty to do with all those boys. Sunny didn't get lonesome for Peter because she saw him in school every day, so you see, everyone was happy.

Then came the day when Sunny finished the eighth grade in our little school and so we sent her to the high school in Long Island, Kansas. During the school week she stayed with some friends of ours and every weekend she came back to us. But soon the high school years were over too and we wanted to send Sunny to college. But she had a different idea. She had met a nice boy, named Joe, in Long Island and they wanted to get married. So, you see, we had a wedding to get ready for. Sunny had her own ideas about that wedding too.

You must remember we lived in the country, miles away from flower shops. So, every wedding in our little church was very much the same. The church owned two large baskets that were filled with paper roses and these came out for every wedding. In one corner of the downstairs supply room there was an old mohair cushion and that was always used for a kneeling bench. But it had been used so much that it was a little tattered and dusty looking. The paper roses, too, had taken the dust of many years.

"I don't want to use any of that old stuff for my wedding," Sunny announced one day. "I'd like real flowers and a different kneeling bench."

"I think we could manage a different bench," Mirandy told her, "but the flowers would be a problem."

"No," Sunny said. "Uncle Josh always called me his little Kansas sunflower and that's what I would like to use for the church decorations. They grow alongside of the road by hundreds and we could pick them ourselves."

At first Mirandy and I said it was a funny idea, but the more we thought about it, the nicer it seemed to us. And what a wedding it turned out to be! Remember, I told you those sunflowers were not

like the big ones they grow for bird seed. They were small, about the size of a big daisy. Well, we picked armfuls of them and put them in the church baskets and tied them to the side of the pews. Aunt Mirandy fixed a new bench too. She used the bench of our old organ and made a beautiful yellow satin cushion for it. We put it

between the baskets of sunflowers. And when I walked with Sunny
down that church aisle, people were amazed to see her dressed in a
very pale yellow dress with a circle of little brown ribbon bows on
the top of her head. She was truly our Kansas sunflower.

The children clapped their hands. It seemed to them that they had been to the wedding.

"Wait a minute, now," Uncle Josh said. "David, I said I would let you answer your own question. Did Mirandy and I have any children of our own?"

David smiled a big, mischievous smile. He thought a minute and then he said, "I guess I would have to say 'yes and no.'"

"You didn't tell us, Uncle Josh," Cee-Cee said. "What did you have to eat at the wedding?"

Uncle Josh blinked his eyes.

"Well, now, I'll be switched,"
he said.

"We had the same thing that you are going to have
for a treat today. "

"Mirandy!"
he called.

"Mirandy, you can dish out the ice cream."

There were whoops and hurrahs from the children.

"Ice cream!
Ice cream!"

they shouted.

"Yes, ice cream," Uncle Josh said. "Homemade ice cream smothered with Kentucky peaches! How about that?"

9
Peter

Uncle Josh sat looking as the children came up the hill. Usually they were almost running, but today they were walking slowly, talking very seriously together. Uncle Josh was pleased about that. He was always glad to have them be a little quiet. It reminded him of his teaching days and how he used to meet the children at the door, after the recess call

bell had rung. "Quiet down, little chickies," he would say. "Leave the vinegar on the playground."

David and Seth were still busy talking together when the five of them arrived.

"My, my," Uncle Josh said. "It seems that the boys are solving big problems today."

"No problems, Uncle Josh," Seth said. "We were just talking about the story you told us last week; the story about

Sunny. But you didn't tell us anything about her brother, Peter. What happened to him?"

"Ho, ho, ho," Uncle Josh laughed.

"You sound just like Santa Claus," David said.

"No, I'm not Santa Claus," Uncle Josh said, "but if you knew Peter you would laugh too. He was some boy! But, come on and sit down and I'll tell you about him."

The children sat down. "This is a special rug, isn't it, Uncle Josh?" Martha asked. "It's really our rug, isn't it?"

"Exactly right," Uncle Josh said. "It's your rug. Your special rug."

And now about Peter. But first of all you must remember that Peter had a problem. Here he was with four other boys, not his brothers, but his cousins. And I think he felt, down deep in his own little heart, that he was not as important to his aunt and uncle as the other boys were. And maybe he was right. I think some of the things he did were done to get a little attention. Well, he got the attention all right, but not always the kind he was looking for. You must remember, as I tell you about him, that Peter was always a willing helper, more so than his cousins. But sometimes that business of wanting to help got him in trouble because he didn't always go about things in the right way. You know, it's not always what you do that is important. HOW you do it is sometimes more important.

One day Peter heard his auntie tell his uncle that it was high time that the fence in the back yard had a coat of paint. Peter decided right then and there that he would be the painter. So the very next day he looked around the barn for brushes and paint and he got busy. But when his uncle drove the horse and wagon into the

yard, he threw up his arms and shouted, "Peter! Peter, put that brush down!"

"I was going to surprise you," Peter said.

"Surprise me?" his uncle shouted. "You surprised me all right, but since when have we ever had a red fence? Barns are red, not fences!"

Uncle got down from his wagon. He knew that Peter had meant to do a good deed but he wondered why Peter never asked first.

"Why did you decide to use red paint?" he asked.

"That's all I could find in the barn," Peter answered.

"We'll have to change it," Uncle said. "Your auntie would never be able to live with a red fence. I'll get you some white paint when I go to town and then you'll have to do it over."

Well, the next week the paint was there and Peter had to get busy, but some of the fun was gone for him. The surprise was gone. And Peter found it very hard to cover that red paint. That part of the fence needed two coats, and as he was working on the last pickets, Uncle came to inspect what Peter had done.

"The red is hard to cover, Uncle," Peter said.

"Oh, I know, I know," Uncle answered. "It comes of not asking first, Peter, but it all looks good, very good, now. Auntie will be happy.

Now, as soon as you are all finished, clean the brush, put the cover tightly on the can, and store it in the barn."

Peter was happy and proud of the good-looking fence.

Now, there was one thing that Peter wanted more than anything else in the whole world, and that was a horse.

"We have a horse," Uncle told him.

"But he's not a riding horse," Peter said.

"I know that," Uncle answered, "but you may ride him."

"But there's no saddle," Peter said.

"You don't need a saddle," Uncle said. "Farm boys ride bare back, and if you ride him you will learn the ways of a horse and then, when you are older, who knows, maybe you can save enough money for a riding horse."

That was fine with Peter. He rode that old horse all over the farm, petted him and talked to him so much that in his own little mind he began to believe that the horse belonged to him.

Then one day Uncle came in from the barn. He looked angry, very angry. He stamped into the kitchen and sat on a chair. Suddenly he put his head in his hands and began to laugh so loud and so long that Auntie thought he would never stop.

"What in the world is wrong with you?" she asked. "First you are angry and now you do nothing but laugh. What is the matter with you?"

Still laughing, Uncle shouted, "Go to the barn. Go to the barn and see for yourself. Somebody painted the horse!" And suddenly Uncle was angry again. "Whoever heard of such a thing! We have a spotted, painted horse!"

Auntie was quiet for several minutes and then she said, rather sadly, "Peter. I think it was Peter."

"That's just what I'm thinking too," Uncle said, "but how can you be sure?"

"Because one day last week he came to me with a picture of a white horse with black spots, and he said, 'Look, Auntie, someday I will have a horse like that.'"

"Well, we have just the opposite. We have a black horse with white spots," Uncle said. "What must I do with that boy?"

Things did not go too well with Peter when he came home. First of all, he didn't want to admit to what he had done.

"I didn't do it," he said. "I didn't do it. I don't know who did it."

"Wait a minute," Uncle said. "Look at your overalls. You look like a spotted boy! You match the horse! Could that be paint?"

Peter knew he was caught. "Yes, Uncle," he said, and then he started to cry. "I wanted him to look like the ponies in pictures," he sobbed. "Don't take it off. Please, don't take it off."

Uncle started laughing again. "It will have to wear off, I guess," he said. And then, quite soberly, he told Peter, "You will go to bed early tonight."

Well, that painted horse was the talk of the farmland. The family used the horse and buggy the next Sunday. When Uncle and Auntie and all of the boys arrived at the church, everyone was laughing. Peter felt a little ashamed and quickly found a place in the back seat until the rest of the family came in.

The minister had a smile on his face, for he had passed the horse on his way to the church.

"There's more to tell about Peter," Uncle Josh said, "but the story will get too long, so we'll save the rest for the next time. I'll tell you a little more about Peter and what became of him."

106

Aunt Mirandy was ready for the children. There was always something a little different. Today she opened the cupboard doors. "Look," she said. And amid squeals of happiness she took out five soup bowls filled with carameled corn. She set them on the kitchen table and gave each child a napkin. "Now," she said, "all little chicks like corn. So, little chicks, peck, peck, peck."

With five children eating carameled corn the kitchen sounded like logs crackling in the fireplace.

"If you eat all that corn," Uncle Josh said, "I'm afraid you'll be hoppin' all the way home."

10
More About Peter

Uncle Josh had an errand to do in the valley. Aunt Miranda had a few things she needed from the village store, so Uncle Josh thought he would surprise the children, meet them at the bottom of the hill, and walk the long way to the cabin with them. Their little faces beamed when they saw him waiting for them and they each struggled to hold his hand.

"We'll take turns," Uncle Josh said. "That's always the fairest way."

Halfway up the hill he stopped. Uncle Josh was out of

breath and a little tired. "Let's sit down for a bit," he said. "There's a lot to look at this time of the year. The colors are so pretty." They sat down, close together.

"Just look at those trees on the hillside on the other side of the valley," Uncle Josh said. "They are all so close together and the autumn colors are really something. Look! Do you all see it?" he asked. "It looks like one giant flower garden."

"What's this?" David asked as he pulled a weed from its root.

"That's a prison," Uncle Josh said. "A prison called a milkweed pod. David, see if you can find an empty one and bring it to me."

There were many right around them so David had no trouble.

"There," Uncle Josh said. "The prison doors are open and all of the prisoners have escaped."

"Who let them out?" David asked.

"A jailor whose name is Mr. Wind," Uncle Josh answered. "He blew so hard that the milkweed pod cracked open. Then he blew again and all the prisoners escaped from their cell. Believe me, that was a crowded jail. But this jail is different from any other, because all the prisoners have the same name—seeds."

Lulu got to her feet and with all the strength her little

hands could muster she picked a flower and brought it to Uncle Josh. "Pretty," she said.

"Yes, that's a pretty flower," Uncle Josh said. Then, passing it to all the children he said, "Use your eyes. Look at it closely. They call it Queen Anne's Lace. Isn't it beautiful? There are many little tiny flowers put together to make one big flower. But, come now. On your feet, everyone. Aunt Mirandy will wonder why it takes us so long."

Once inside of the the little cabin, the children reminded Uncle Josh that he was going to finish the story about Peter.

Well, now, Peter had his spotted horse. He had gotten used to riding bareback, but oh, how he wanted to be a cowboy, and how he longed for a cowboy pony and cowboy clothes, especially a hat and the boots. The boots, he knew, were out of the question, but he had an idea for the hat. Uncle wore a black hat to church on Sunday and Peter thought that if he rolled the sides of the brim maybe it would look like a cowboy hat. It was up on a high shelf in Uncle's bedroom but he could reach it, for by this time Peter was twelve years old. So, when he was sure everyone was out of the house he helped himself to Uncle's hat. He carried it into the barn and hid it in a dark corner.

Each day he went to his secret hiding place and rolled and rolled the stiff brim. Then he would put it on his head and scrunch himself up in the corner and say, "Whoa! Whoa!" In his own mind, you see, he was a riding cowboy because he had a cowboy hat. He would liked to have put it on his head and then ridden his horse, but he knew that was out of the question, for his cousins would surely see it and no one must know that he had taken Uncle's Sunday hat.

But before too many days had passed, it was Sunday, and when everyone was ready to go to church and the boys had hitched the spotted horse to the buggy, Uncle went to the shelf for his hat. What? No hat! He called to Auntie, "Where did you put my hat?"

"On the shelf where I always put it," she called back.

"It's not here," Uncle said.

Auntie came to the room, expecting to find it exactly where she had put it, but there was no hat. "That's funny," she said. "I'll ask the boys."

She called out of the open window. "Boys! Boys, has anyone seen Papa's Sunday hat?"

Of course, not one had, not even Peter!

For a farmer to come to a Sunday church service without a hat was a terrible thing, people thought, and Uncle was upset. He was even more upset when he arrived at the church and the other farmers teased him about it.

"Where's your hat, Charlie?" one farmer said. "Are you saving it for your spotted horse to wear? On a hot summer day a horse can use a hat."

During the coming week Auntie almost turned the house upside down looking for the hat that had disappeared so strangely. This time nobody even suspected Peter. After all, what would Peter possibly want with Uncle's Sunday hat?

Toward the end of the week Uncle made a trip to the city and bought himself a new one, while the old one with its rolled-up brim stayed hidden in the barn. Peter played his game of cowboy there every day.

Each day his longing to be a cowboy grew stronger. In school he drew cowboy pictures and wrote cowboy stories. At home he talked on and on about the cowboys and how he hoped to be one some day.

Auntie and Uncle grew a little tired of hearing cowboy talk all the time. One day Uncle put down the newspaper he was reading and he said to Peter, "Do you know that cowboys work? Do you think a cowboy does nothing all day except ride on a pony and put on the beautiful clothes you see him wear in the magazine pictures? A cowboy leads a rough, hard life!"

"Doing what?" Peter asked.

"Lots of things," Uncle said. "Every day the cowboys are out on the range rounding up the cattle and bringing them back to the corral. Sometimes, if the cattle are grazing far out on the range they stay with them for several days. Then the chuck wagon and the cook go along and the cowboys have to eat out-of-doors."

"Oh, I'd like that," Peter said.

"Well," Uncle said. "How would you like branding the calves and the colts? Would you like to take the red hot branding iron and burn a pattern on to those poor animals?"

"Why do they do that?" Peter asked.

"Because each ranch has an iron of a different shape and it helps the cowboys to know where the animals belong. It helps to prevent stealing the cattle too. And how would you like knocking a sheep over and roping his legs together and then shearing off his wool?"

"I could get used to it," Peter said.

"Then there's the breaking in of the colts. That's not an easy job. A colt has to learn to allow a cowboy on his back. First the colt is led round and round the corral for several days. Then he is covered with a folded blanket so that he can get used to something on his back. Next comes a saddle, which is a little heavier. And finally a cowboy

tries to ride him. But oh, how the colt kicks his hind legs into the air. Sometimes he succeeds in throwing the cowboy to the ground. Now, how would you like that?"

Peter smiled. "I would get used to that too," he said.

Uncle gave up trying to convince Peter, but when Peter had

gone to bed Uncle talked a few things over with Auntie. "Maybe," he said, "we should put Peter on a ranch for the summer."

"Where?" Auntie asked.

"With my friend, Jerry Carlton, in Colorado. He owns the JERRY C ranch there and he might be willing to take Peter. He knew

Peter's father and mother. But say nothing to Peter about it. I must first find out what Jerry has to say."

Uncle lost no time in writing to Jerry Carlton and when a letter came back saying that he could use a young boy for watering the horses and many other little things, Uncle was happy.

When evening came and they were sitting in the living room, Uncle asked Peter, "How would you like to spend the summer on a ranch in Colorado?"

Peter jumped from his chair, and the questions flew. "When? Where? With whom? How come? Who said so?"

Uncle explained, and from that spring day until school ended, Peter thought about very little besides the ranch. He even forgot about the hat in the corner of the barn and he pictured himself as a real cowboy, boots, chaps, a hat and the whole outfit.

When all of the arrangements with Mr. Carlton had been made and the last school-bell had rung, Peter was put on the train and assured that Mr. Carlton would meet him at the depot in Colorado and then drive him to the ranch. Auntie was a little unhappy when she said goodbye to Peter and Uncle was a little scared. What if Peter didn't like it after all? What if he would be homesick?

But when the short letters from Peter came there was no sign of homesickness. All the cowboys were his friends, he said, and he had his own special pony to ride. And when Uncle wrote and asked him if he was wearing those fancy cowboy clothes, Peter wrote back that he was wearing the same thing the other cowboys were wearing—blue jeans. But he did have a cowboy hat that one of the men had given him.

For Peter the time passed all too quickly and when he came home to begin school again he had a hard time keeping his mind on his school work. That summer on the JERRY C ranch was only the beginning for Peter. He went back every summer.

"What happened about Uncle's Sunday hat?" Seth asked.

Uncle Josh laughed. "Would you believe it?" he said. "One day the family dog found it in the corner of the barn and brought it out and played with it in the yard. So from that day on the poor dog got the blame for taking the hat out of the house and hiding it."

"Where is Peter now?" Martha asked.

"Oh, Peter is grown up and married," Uncle Josh said. "He has two little cowboys of his own and one little cowgirl. And he has a ranch of his very own in Colorado, not too many miles from the JERRY C. On that ranch he raises some very special horses. Can you guess what kind?"

"Spotted ones, spotted ones," the children shouted.

Uncle Josh smiled a big smile and the children knew that their guess was right.

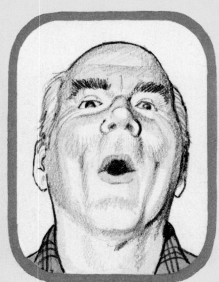